Monkey Business

To Katie, my love, and to my little chums
Calla, Sadie, Matthew and Harriet.

Many thanks to Jane F., Mike F. and Jenny C.

Kids Can Press acknowledges the financial support of the Government of
Ontario, through the Ontario Media Development Corporation's Ontario Book Initiative;
the Ontario Arts Council; the Canada Council for the Arts; and the Government
of Canada, through the BPIDP, for our publishing activity.

Published in Canada by
Kids Can Press Ltd.
29 Birch Avenue
Toronto, ON   M4V 1E2

Published in the U.S. by
Kids Can Press Ltd.
2250 Military Road
Tonawanda, NY   14150

www.kidscanpress.com

The artwork in this book was rendered in watercolor, colored pencil and gouache.
The text is set in CrudFont.

Edited by Tara Walker
Designed by Julia Naimska
Printed and bound in China

This book is smyth sewn casebound.

CM 04   0 9 8 7 6 5 4 3 2

National Library of Canada Cataloguing in Publication Data

Edwards, Wallace

Monkey business / Wallace Edwards.

ISBN 1-55337-462-2 (bound)

1. English language — Idioms — Juvenile literature.
I. Title.

PE1460.E48 2004   j428   C2004-900410-7

Kids Can Press is a ℓ©ⲅ∪s™ Entertainment company

Monkey Business

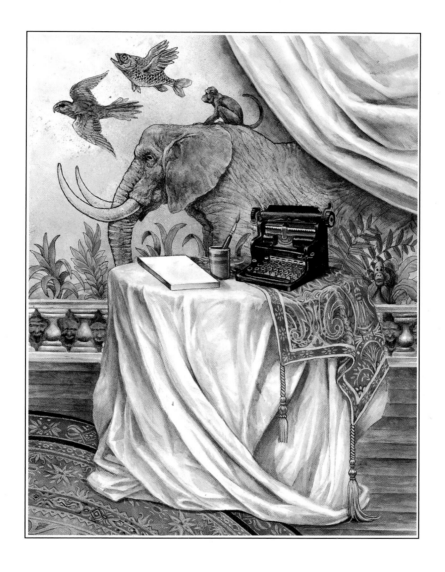

Wallace Edwards

Kids Can Press

IDIOM: a group of words whose meaning cannot be understood from the meaning of the individual words; an expression, peculiar to a specific language, that cannot be translated literally

Even in a serious meeting, Professor Apeson sensed there might be monkey business going on.

When he was on the ball, there was no
limit to what King Pigglebottom could do.

It was cold and wet outside, but Gavin felt as snug as a bug in a rug.

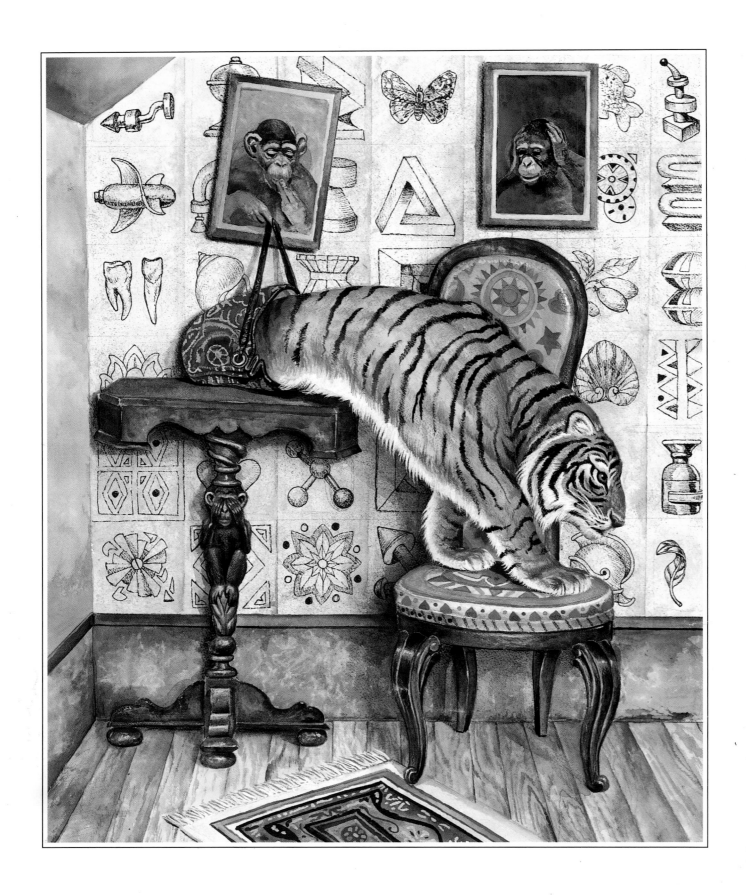

Although Mumford had promised not to gossip, he let the cat out of the bag.

"Not again," sighed Owen. "It isn't easy being a bull in a china shop."

Eloise had a craving for snails, but she accidentally opened a can of worms.

Phil had no formal musical training,
so he learned to play by ear.

Quentin could always be counted on
to rise to the occasion.

Sometimes, thought Camellia, it's
better to show your true colors.

Forbes had no intention of sharing his cupcake — he had a real sweet tooth.

When it was time to deliver, Peg laid
it on the line.

"'Tis a dog-eat-dog world," mused Reginald,
reflecting on his life of hard-won luxury.

Having departed from her usual pattern,
Isadora seemed a little off-the-wall.

The MacRhino brothers, Angus and Skip, would often lock horns over who got to play the pipes.

As an artist, Nash was constantly looking for things to sink his teeth into.

While doing his famous wiggly dance,
the Amazing Schuman always tried to
put his best foot forward.

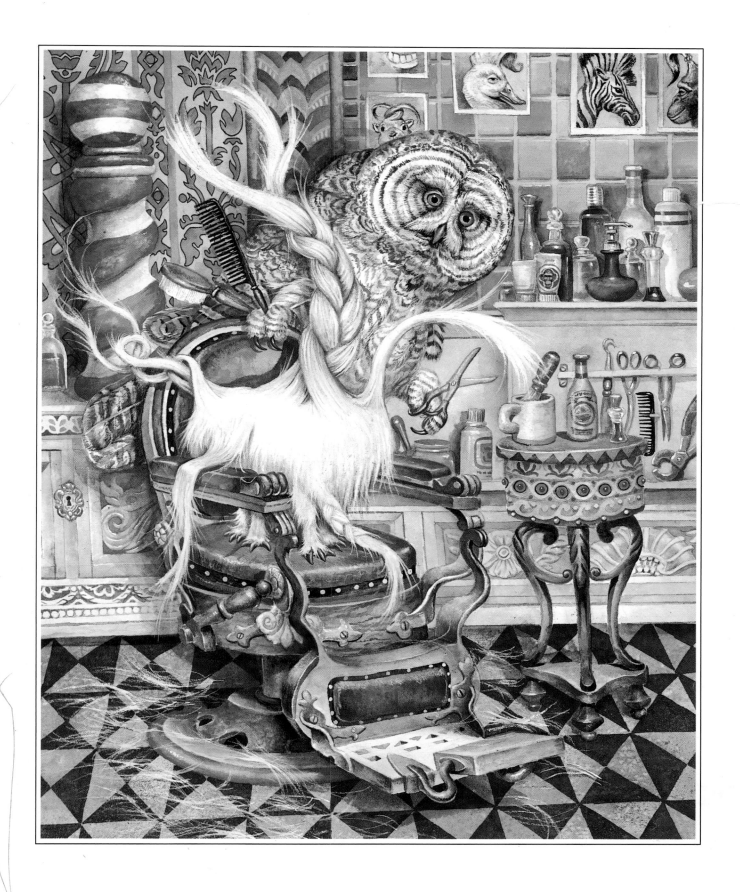

Despite his great skill as a barber,
Hank couldn't make heads or tails out
of some of his customers.

Snowflake had a strange feeling that someone was playing cat and mouse with her.

Willy seemed to attract misfortune,
but Bill was a lucky duck.

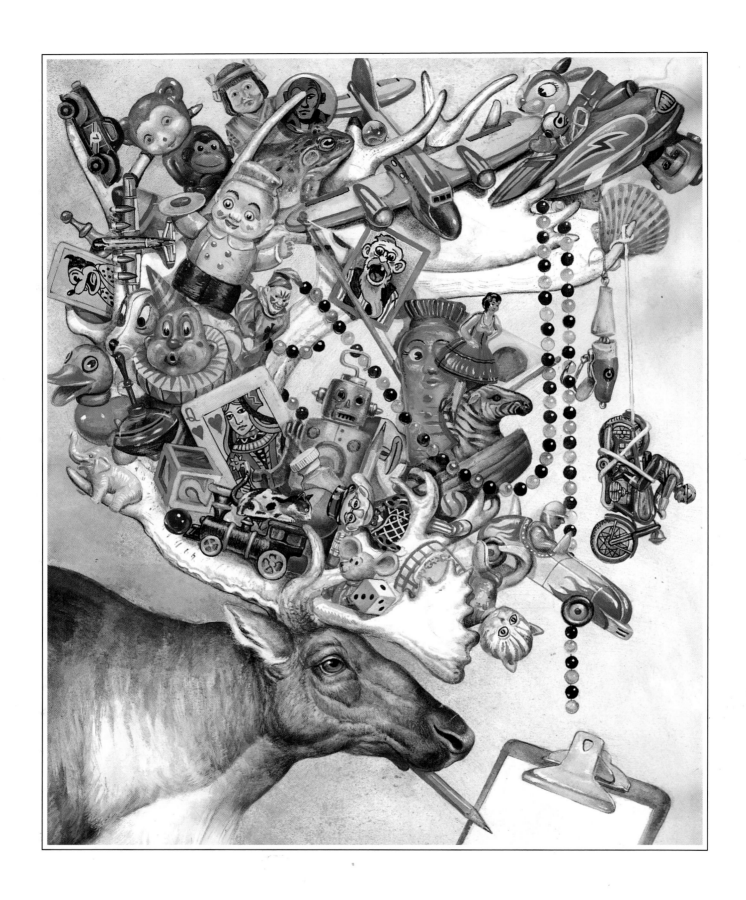

Byron had a lot on his mind, yet he couldn't think of a word to write.

Win or lose, when Bluebell raced Big
Daddy Jim she always had a whale
of a ride.

Although he blended in with the gang, Darnell was just a wolf in sheep's clothing.

When she realized she'd taken a wrong turn Gloria felt like a fish out of water.

After saying she wouldn't be hurry
if she missed lunch, Paige ended up
eating her words.

Every time the Bobzee twins bounced by, Old Zeke was reminded that he wasn't a spring chicken anymore.

Wally knew it was time
to draw things to a close.

Enough Monkeying Around!

Here's What It Means ...

BULL IN A CHINA SHOP: a clumsy or rough person who is around breakable things; a thoughtless person

CAN'T MAKE HEADS OR TAILS OUT OF: to be unable to understand someone or something

DOG-EAT-DOG: fiercely competitive; a situation in which you have to be ruthless in order to survive or succeed

DRAW THINGS TO A CLOSE: to end or finish

EAT YOUR WORDS: to have to take back what you said; to admit that you were wrong

FISH OUT OF WATER: someone who is in unfamiliar or uncomfortable surroundings; someone who doesn't fit in or is awkward or helpless in a situation

HAVE A LOT ON YOUR MIND: to have many things to think or worry about

LAY IT ON THE LINE: to speak firmly and directly about something

LET THE CAT OUT OF THE BAG: to give away a secret

LOCK HORNS: to disagree or argue

LUCKY DUCK: a fortunate person

MONKEY BUSINESS: silly, playful or foolish behavior; mischievous, dishonest or illegal activities

OFF-THE-WALL: odd or unusual

ON THE BALL: alert, effective, efficient

OPEN A CAN OF WORMS: to cause trouble; to bring up a problem that will lead to more problems

PLAY BY EAR: to play a tune after hearing it rather than by reading musical notes; to improvise

PLAY CAT AND MOUSE: to tease or fool someone by pretending to let her go free, then catching her again

PUT YOUR BEST FOOT FORWARD: to do or show your best; to try to make a good impression

RISE TO THE OCCASION: to meet a challenge; to try hard to do a task

SHOW YOUR TRUE COLORS: to reveal what you are really like or what you are really thinking

SINK YOUR TEETH INTO: to take a bite of something; to get a chance to do or learn something challenging

SNUG AS A BUG IN A RUG: cozy and comfortable

SPRING CHICKEN: a young person

SWEET TOOTH: a liking for sweet foods such as candy, cake or chocolate

WHALE OF A RIDE: an exciting or enjoyable experience

WOLF IN SHEEP'S CLOTHING: an enemy pretending to be a friend; something dangerous disguised as something harmless